THE DR. CAGE CHRONICLES: MEMOIRS OF A SEX THERAPIST

How I Got Here

The Dr. Cage Chronicles: Memoirs of a Sex Therapist

How I Got Here

Grayson Ace

4 Horsemen
Publications, Inc.

Dedicated to
all the boys
who have
mistakenly
broken my

heart.

PROLOGUE

*H*i. I'm Hunter Cage. Well, actually, it's Dr. Hunter Cage. I'm a Sex Therapist, and I specialize in assisting gay men cope with their desires and fantasies and help them to understand why they are the way they are. Everyone thinks one of two things: a gay man chooses to be gay, or he was born gay. In reality, there could be so many other things that cause a man to be gay.

I grew up in a very small town in rural Pennsylvania called Intercourse. No, I couldn't make that up if I tried. Let's just say my upbringing greatly shaped who I am today, but we will get more into those details a bit later.

I opened my practice in the Castro District of San Francisco a few years back. I wanted to go to an area where I could make the biggest impact on gay men and figured: what better place to do this than the gay capital of the U.S.? My office sits on a very busy street, but I had a reflective covering installed on all of the windows, allowing for privacy during therapy sessions. These windows have many stories to tell.

These chronicles will walk you through the lives and events of many of my patients—as well as myself—all names and locations being changed to protect their privacy. But before we get into any sessions, it's important to take you back to where things all began and show you what shaped me, Dr. Cage.

Chapter 1

INTERCOURSE, PA

Intercourse is a small rural town about two hours outside of Philadelphia. It's one of those towns where a gay man wouldn't be caught dead in any type of public display of affection. Quite honestly, it's the type of town you would imagine being the backdrop of many hate crimes.

I grew up in a pretty average white-collar American family. My dad worked for a union fiberglass company—I think he may have been the foreman or union steward—one of those important positions. He was very proud to be a union member, but even prouder to be an American. He always worked on special projects on Saturday mornings to get overtime.

My mom didn't work, except on Sundays, where she would teach Bible lessons to the children at church. After church though, she would join her friends for her weekly book club meetings. I always wanted to go with her, but she said the book topics would bore me. My brothers and I were her world, and there wasn't anything that she wouldn't do for us.

My parents seemed to have a perfect marriage. Either that, or they were really good at hiding their problems from us. I have two brothers. Rocky is two years older than I am. He was a typical jock. He worked out every night and had the perfect muscles to show for it. I swear my mom would catch him almost weekly sneaking a girl into his room.

Harry is two years younger than I am. He was a bit of a dork and super shy. He aspired to work for a union just like my dad and would pretend to build machines just to have something to relate to my dad.

My brothers and I didn't spend a lot of time with each other because we really didn't have anything in common. Rocky was always chasing girls, and Harry would read books about machinery. We didn't have any air conditioning in the house, and the summers could get pretty hot, so I would spend the majority of my time in the basement family room.

I remember walking down into the basement on days and seeing my dad in the corner behind the built-in bar. His back was facing me and apparently he didn't hear me come down the stairs, which I'm not sure how. There was a shelf built into the wall behind the bar where the water meter was, and I noticed him reaching up into the rafters, but there wasn't anything in his hands when he pulled them down.

He turned around, and I quickly acted like I wasn't paying attention and said, "Hey dad, aren't you supposed to be at work?"

He looked at me with a bit of a grin and responded, "Yeah son, I'm about to go in." Of course he was about to go in–it was Saturday, so time for that overtime.

My dad walked up the stairs, and I sat down on the couch, staring at the corner behind the bar. I was dying to know what was up in the rafters, but I knew I needed to wait until he left. A few minutes later, I head his truck pull out of the driveway. I darted for the corner and started looking up into the rafters. I couldn't see anything, and I was too short to reach up there, so I stood on one of the bar shelves and hung onto the molding of the wall, reaching my hands into a small dark crevice in the rafter. I was a little hesitant, not knowing if something would jump out and bite me. I felt around for about ten seconds when my hand landed on something plastic.

"Bingo!" I thought. What was dad hiding? I grabbed onto the plastic, and to my surprise, pulled out a VHS tape that had a faded label on it. I squinted to be able to read the faded print only to make out the word "Ebony."

Chapter 2

EBONY

*N*ow I had to find out what was so secretive about this tape that my dad had to hide it rather than just keep it with all the Disney VHS tapes on the bookshelf. I turned on the TV and popped the video tape into the VCR. Naturally, there were lines going through the TV, so I gave the top of the VCR a few firm slams with my fist and the lines went away. The typical movie things popped up on the screen–piracy warnings from the FBI that no one paid attention to, a few movie credits, and an advertisement for something called "The Rabbit," which I didn't quite understand.

After the advertisement, a video popped up with two naked girls on the screen, and one was holding a telephone. A scrolling bar appeared at the bottom of the screen that read "For a good time call…" with some 1-900 number after it. At this point, I understood why my dad wasn't keeping this video tape with the rest of the Disney movies. I shot out of my seat and ran over to the television to turn it away from the small basement windows in fear that someone would see what I was watching. I sat back down on the couch, excited, nervous, and a little scared, because I knew what I was about to witness, and I was terrified that I would get in trouble.

The 1-900 advertisement was over, and I only assume that character of "Ebony" is whom I was now seeing on the screen. She was a naked black woman with long dark hair and the biggest tits that I had ever seen. She was sitting on a chair by herself when a fully dressed man walked over. Ebony remained on the chair, and the man was standing right in front of her. She grabbed his belt and took it off and then unbuttoned and unzipped his pants. She then pulled out his enormously erect cock and started sucking on it. I had never seen a cock so big. As she was sucking on his cock, she was also stoking it with her hands.

I looked down at my own cock because it started moving on its own. I would sometimes wake up with a hard cock, and it would sometimes get hard during math class, but I realized that what I was watching on the video was causing it to grow.

How cool!

I pulled off my gym shorts and sat there with my hard cock hanging out and just kind of moved it back and forth. I kept watching the movie. Right after I let my own cock out of my shorts, the man in the video took off his shirt and pants and picked Ebony up off the chair. He threw her down on the bed and put his cock inside of her vagina and began fucking her really hard. Ebony started screaming so loudly that I had to get up and turn the volume down on the tv.

The man fucked Ebony for about fifteen minutes in a bunch of different positions. I assumed the movie was over when he got off the bed, but there was more. Ebony also got off the bed and got down on her knees in front of the man's cock, and the man started stroking his own cock. I thought that was an interesting move and didn't understand why he wouldn't just keep fucking her. I figured if he was doing that to himself that I might as well try it out myself as well, so I started stroking my own cock.

Holy fuck.

That was the best feeling in the world. I remember lying back on the couch and stroking my cock while I watched the man stroke his.

A million thoughts were racing through my head while I was stroking my cock: Why didn't I start doing this years ago? I wonder if my dad does this. My brothers? Oh, I need to tell Harry about this!

Then I started focusing on the man's cock again, wondering if mine would ever be as big as his, and if I'd ever get to fuck a big titty girl like Ebony. I kept stroking on my cock when the man let out of loud grunting sound. Just then a bunch of white, milky looking liquid came out of the head of his cock, almost like water coming out of a fire hose. He shot that liquid all over Ebony's face and in her mouth, pulled on his pants, grabbed his shirt, and walked out of the bedroom.

The tv screen went black, but I kept stroking my cock because it felt so good. About thirty seconds later, I started to feel a bit of a burning sensation in my cock, and the feeling was getting deeper. I kept stroking it and knew I was about to let out a loud grunting sound just like the man did when he was stroking his cock. Then, it happened. That white, milky liquid shot out of the hole in the head of my cock all over my white t-shirt. I instantly felt a sense of relief and realized why the man made the loud grunting sound. It finally happened. I just had my first orgasm.

There was now white liquid all over my t-shirt. I took it off and rolled it up in a ball. I grabbed my shorts and put them back on. I got the rewound video out of the VCR and carefully placed it back in my dad's hiding spot. I ran to the top of the stairs and slowly opened the door to see if anyone was in the kitchen. The coast was clear, so I threw my balled-up shirt in the garbage can and ran to my bedroom as fast as I could. I slammed the door shut behind me and locked it and jumped right into bed. I laid there for a minute, thinking about what had just happened and how good it felt. I pulled my shorts back down, grabbed my cock, and went for round two. I had just found my new hobby.

Chapter 3

ABBY

Literally over the next couple of years, I spent all of my free time masturbating. It was the greatest feeling in the world, and sometimes I would do it four or five times a day. My dad had a couple other video tapes in the basement that proved to be a lot of help, but none were ever as good as Ebony was.

Masturbating became my new way to release all the built-up energy I had. Living in Pennsylvania was tough, and there really wasn't a whole lot to do, especially in Intercourse, so masturbating was really the only thing I could think to do when I was bored. Plus, it gave me an awesome feeling, although the mess it left was a bit of a downer.

Rocky would make fun of me because he had caught me several times jerking off, whether in the shower or in my room. One time he snuck in the bathroom and dumped a bucket of cold water over the shower curtain while I was lying in the bathtub jerking off. I always thought it was weird that he seemed to know whenever I had my hard cock in my hand. One time, he burst through my bedroom door to let me know dinner was ready. Literally the minute he opened my door, I shot my load all over my chest. We both just kind of looked at each other, neither of us seeming to be embarrassed by what had just happened. He grinned, said, "Dinner's ready," shut my door, and walked away. His reaction was a bit strange, but with a sex drive like his, I'm sure he and his buddies sit around jerking off together all the time like it's no big deal.

I grabbed a balled-up t-shirt out of my bottom dresser drawer and wiped the cum off my chest. I pulled up my shorts and threw on a new shirt and walked out of my bedroom to join my family for dinner. I was starving, probably from the amount of work that I had just accomplished. Masturbating always took a lot of energy out of me, and I was always hungry afterwards. I sat down so quickly I didn't even notice the blonde girl sitting across from me.

I did, however, notice her huge tits that practically sat on the table in front of her dinner plate. Just as I took my eyes away from her tits to look at my brother, she said, "Hi, I'm Abby."

"Hi, I'm Hunter," I responded. I didn't really take note of her name because I figured within a week my brother would have someone different sitting at the dinner table with us anyway. Girls were like a revolving door to him, and he never seemed to bring the same one over more than five times. They never seemed to leave unhappy though.

While we were eating dinner, Rocky's phone started going off from text messages. My mom had a rule that we weren't allowed to have our cell phones at the table during meals. Rocky picked up the phone to look at the message and my mom snapped. One thing you never wanted to do was make my mom angry. I don't even know if I had ever seen her angry, but I knew you didn't want to get her to that level. She immediately took Rocky's phone and threw it across the room. There was a bucket of water on the floor in the corner of the dining room that was catching water that was dripping from the ceiling from a storm the night before.

Sure enough, the phone landed right in the bucket.

Rocky jumped out of his chair and ran over to grab it, yelling a bunch of profanities along the way. As he grabbed his phone out of the water, the bucket tipped over, sending water all across the dining room floor. My dad stood up so quickly that his chair had to have flown six feet behind him. Dad started yelling. Rocky started yelling louder. My mother sat at the end of the table clutching her pearls, and I just kept eating my mashed potatoes.

Rocky did the typical "I hate all of you" and went running off to his room, but surprisingly, Abby didn't follow him. She sat there staring at me for a minute, which was little creepy, so I said, "I'm finished" and got up out of my chair to go down into the basement and watch a movie. As I was walking away, I heard Abby say, "I'll help you clear the table Mrs. Cage."

I got down into the basement and started walking over to the corner to grab Ebony out of her hiding spot. With all the commotion from tonight, though, I was afraid one of my parents would end up in the basement wanting to watch tv with me, so I just turned on ESPN and started watching highlights from the game. The couch was old and not very comfortable, so I grabbed a bunch of pillows and blankets and made myself a bit of a makeshift bed on the floor in front of the couch. It was a hot night, so I had planned on sleeping down there anyway.

About 15 minutes after I got into the basement, I heard the door at the top of the stairs open, and I figured it was my dad coming down to watch tv with me. I was quite surprised when the first thing I saw walk around the corner from the staircase was Abby. There she was, with her long blonde hair and those enormous tits. I don't think I had ever seen tits so big on such a small girl.

She walked in the room and asked if she could watch tv with me. I shrugged my shoulders at her and said, "I guess." I really didn't want her down there with me because I was starting to get in the mood to jerk off. It was getting late, so I figured at that point my parents wouldn't be joining me. She wasn't going to be interested in the game anyways, so it's not like she'd be staying down there very long.

I asked her what Rocky was doing and she said that he was sitting in his room pouting about his broken iPhone, and she really wasn't in the mood to listen to him bitch. She then started talking to me about how much of an asshole my brother is, as if I didn't already know that. If only she knew about the five other girls that he had brought back to the house over the past two weeks.

As she continued to complain about my brother, she pulled up the blanket that I was under and laid down next to me, covering herself with the blanket. She said she was cold and wanted to get closer to me to stay warm, and since I was lying on my side to be able to see the tv, she backed her ass right into my dick. I immediately looked up at the sky and closed my eyes and started thinking about something–anything–to keep myself from getting a boner.

What was happening? Why was my brother's girlfriend under the blanket with me? Why did she just back her ass right up into my junk? It was too late. I could already feel my cock growing hard, and it was growing fast.

I heard Abby let out a chuckle, and she said, "What's going on back there?"

Just as she said that, she reached her hand backwards and felt for my cock. The minute she brushed the head of my cock, it started throbbing, and I swear it was about to rip right through my shorts. Naturally, I was wearing gym shorts and no underwear, so the feeling of her hand brushing against my cock was extra sensitive.

She chuckled again and said, "Did I do this to you?"

I started to apologize and began to turn away when Abby turned over and was now facing me. She stopped rubbing my cock through the outside of my shorts, and instead pulled the front of my shorts down, letting my cock pop out freely and at full attention.

She grabbed onto my cock and started slowly rubbing it.

Holy shit.

How could this feel so amazing and feel even better than when I'm doing it by myself? She got a little closer to me and pressed her lips against mine, and then pushed her tongue through my closed lips until it was caressing mine.

This was really happening. My brother's girlfriend, or whatever she was, was stroking my cock and making out with me.

I grabbed her tits and started moving my hand all over them. She was wearing a tank top, so it left for pretty easy access. I pulled her top to the side so I could get to her nipples, and I started rubbing my fingers over her nipples while she was still stroking my cock.

I stopped kissing her and moved my mouth onto her nipples. Ever since watching Ebony, I had wanted to suck on some nice hard nipples. I began sucking on them like a. baby bottle, and she took my hand and put it down into her pants.

There it was. I was actually experiencing what it felt like to rub a vagina.

She guided my fingers for a bit and held onto my hand while I was rubbing her clit, and she started kissing me again while still stroking my cock. This chick hadn't let go of my cock the entire time. She didn't even loosen her grip. At one point, she even told me that my cock was bigger that Rocky's, which I was shocked to hear.

I rubbed on the outside of her mons for a few minutes, and then decided to lift up her panties so I could really get in there. I put one finger inside her vagina, and she let out a loud moan. After a minute, I put a second one in there and started thrusting it in and out just like I had seen the guy do to Ebony. My fingers were getting really wet, and this was becoming the greatest night of my life. After a couple of minutes, Abby pulled my fingers out of her vagina, and she pushed my head back on the pillow so I was lying flat. I wasn't quite sure what was about to happen, but based on what had already occurred, I was ready to find out.

I was lying there on my back, my hard cock standing straight up in the air, and Abby kind of lifted herself up from the position she was lying in and started going toward my legs. She went down in front of me and got in between my leg so that she was facing me. She grabbed the base of my cock and started licking the head with her tongue. I grabbed my face because I really didn't know what was happening, and I couldn't even believe it. She twirled her tongue around the tip of my cock for about five seconds and then just swallowed the entire thing.

Wow, this is what a blowjob felt like. At first, she was sucking it pretty slowly, going all the way down to the base of my cock with her lips, gagging a little bit, and then coming back up to the head. I could feel her tongue moving all over my cock as she was going up and down on it. She would start going a little faster, bouncing her head up and down, and sometimes she would even stroke my cock at the same time she was sucking it. That felt the best, and at one point, I thought she was going to make me cum, so I grabbed her head and pulled her mouth off my dick because I wasn't ready to cum.

I pulled her head up toward mine and started making out with her again. She never let go of my cock and kept stroking it for the next 30 seconds while we continued to make out. She went back down to my cock and wrapped her lips around it, and I knew what she wanted. She started bobbing her head up and down, sucking on my dick while she was stroking my shaft up and down. She started going faster, and I knew I was about to shoot my load all over.

I said, "I'm about to cum," thinking that she would take her mouth off my cock and just jerk me off, but she didn't stop. She kept on sucking my cock like it was going to be the last cock she had in her mouth. Or maybe mine really was that much better than my brother's. I must have said "I'm going to cum" two or three more times, but she still didn't stop.

And then it happened.

I started shooting my load into her mouth, and she just kept on sucking and stroking it. I must have cum for a solid ten seconds, and with every palpitation of my body and my cock, more and more cum shot into her mouth. The whole time I was cumming, she never stopped stroking or sucking on my cock. At this point, there was cum starting to come out of her mouth and down my cock, and I didn't even care. This was by far the hottest experience I had ever had.

She took her mouth off my cock and let go of it from her death grip and made a loud gulping sound. She was actually swallowing my cum. I didn't even know that was a thing, but she swallowed all of it, except for what had dripped back down onto my pelvis, and then just let out a big smile. I wasn't really sure what was supposed to happen next. She grabbed the blanket and wiped off her mouth, gave me a kiss on the cheek, and ran upstairs. I sat up, pulled my shorts up and thought to myself, "What the fuck just happened?"

I knew one thing for sure– I was about to start jerking off a whole lot more.

Chapter 4

LOSING THE V CARD

I remember losing my virginity like it was yesterday, although it really isn't that exciting of a story.

Most of our vacations were spent visiting family out of town; we never really got to go to any places that were actually cool and exciting. One summer we went to visit some family in Minnesota. Naturally, my dad didn't join us because he never wanted to take any time off of work. So, it was just my brothers, my mom, and me.

26

We spent nearly two days in the car to get there, and it was horrible. My mom was scared of flying, so that was entirely out of the question. Once we got to Minnesota, we basically spend the week just hanging out at my aunt's house. They owned a farm, so it was a huge piece of property that seemed to go on for miles. We would go out into the fields on the quads and chase around the horses. At night, we would usually build a fire and just sit around and talk.

That Saturday was the 4th of July, and my family was throwing a big picnic. All of my cousins showed up with their families, and a bunch of their friends were there as well. Apparently, it was a big tradition for them to have this huge picnic, and my uncle would attempt to do an exhilarating firework display that—shockingly—ended up sucking.

I was sitting at a picnic table eating my hot dog and macaroni salad, and one of my cousin's friends sat down next to me. To this day, I still can't remember her name, so let's just call her Jane. Jane was a few years older than I was with long blonde hair and pretty small tits. She asked me where I was from, how I liked Minnesota, and if I played any sports.

I could tell she must have been as bored as I was and was just trying to make small talk. We sat there and talked for about ten minutes, and then she asked me if I wanted to go for a walk. I really didn't want to go anywhere. I was tired and being lazy, and I actually wanted to go get another hot dog. But fuck it–I figured if we went for this walk maybe we'd end up making out or something.

We started walking away from the picnic and moved across the property parallel to the corn field. I thought for sure one of my brothers would come running after me asking where we were going. Jane did most of the talking. I wasn't really paying any attention to what she was saying, but I just kind of kept nodding my head and agreeing with her. After walking for about fifteen minutes, we stumbled upon some old-looking shack. It was basically a shed, but it had a window and a little front porch. Jane preceded to open the door and walk inside, but I stayed outside. She turned around and looked at me and asked if I was scared to come in. I shook my head and followed her inside.

As soon as I got inside, she closed the door behind me, walked up to me and grabbed my dick through my shorts. I was shocked that she did this, but definitely not mad. Before I could even say anything, she had her tongue down my throat and was making out with me. It kind of reminded me of the time I was with Abby in the basement. We made out for a few minutes while she continued rubbing my dick, which was as hard as a rock at this point. I started playing with her small tits, and I wanted to go down towards her vagina, but I was waiting for her to make the move.

All of the sudden, she let go of my dick, dropped to her knees, and ripped my shorts down as fast as she could. My natural reaction was to try and grab them to prevent my dick from flying out, but I was too late. My hard dick was already in her mouth, and she was bobbing her head back and forth on it. This girl must have been a pro, or she'd sucked a lot of cock because this felt so much better than Abby. At one point, she was even able to put my entire dick in her mouth, which made me smile when she started gagging. She put her hands on my thighs and pushed me back a little bit to get my cock out of her mouth. My dick was covered in her saliva, and it was dripping out of her mouth. She ran her arm across her mouth to wipe it off, looked up at me, and said, "I want you to fuck me."

I had no clue what to do or say.

I wanted to fuck her, but this wasn't how I had imagined losing my virginity. I didn't have a condom. I didn't know if she had a condom. What if she got pregnant? I was thinking a million things, and all I said to her was "okay."

Jane got up off her knees and pulled her shorts and panties down. There was a table right next to us, and she spun around and sat up on the table. She pulled me over to her, licked her fingers and wiped her pussy to get it wet. She grabbed my dick and slowly put it inside of her pussy. This was such a more intense feeling than getting my dick sucked. As soon as my dick was all the way inside of her, I looked up at the ceiling and let out a loud moan. I knew what to do from watching the guy do it to Ebony, so I began. I started thrusting my dick in and out of her vagina really fast. She was moaning like someone who just had their insides ripped out. The faster I went, the louder she got. Even if I went slower, she was still pretty loud.

I could tell I was about to cum and asked her where I should finish. At that moment, she pushed my chest so that my cock would fall out of her pussy, and she quickly got down off the table and onto her knees. She put my dick in her mouth for a few seconds and then took it out and was jerking it right in front of her face. Not even five seconds of her jerking it, and I was shooting my load all over her face.

She kept opening her mouth to catch some of it and then would spit it back out. There's no way my family didn't hear me at this point because I was making the loudest moan I had ever made. She put my dick back in her mouth and fuck if she didn't suck it dry. She wiped her face off with her panties and threw them in the corner. She pulled her shorts back up, looked at me, said "Thank you," and ran back to the party.

I went over into the corner and grabbed her panties. I needed something to wipe my dick off with. I wiped it off, put my shorts back back, and walked out of the shack to start going back to the party. I learned a valuable lesson that day: always say yes when someone asks you to go on a walk.

Chapter 5

ELISSA

I've really only ever had one girlfriend in my life. Her name was Elissa, and she was the most gorgeous brunette I had ever laid eyes on. She came from a pretty high class family, and grew up in the same town I did. Her mom didn't work and was the best damn cook I've ever met. She would often invite my entire family over for these over-the-top meals. What I considered to be Thanksgiving dinner, they considered to be a typical Wednesday night. Her dad was in the Army, but you'd never know from looking at him. He was tall and skinny and was very kind. I took a strong liking to her dad, and even went on a few "guy trips" with him and her brothers.

I really wanted to have sex with Elissa shortly after we started dating, but she was a virgin and wanted to wait for a while. She was afraid it would hurt and was afraid her parents would find out. Her mom would often joke around and say things like "I'll know that Elissa is having sex when she starts using tampons." (Apparently, she would only wear pads). I guess they thought this was funny to joke about, but it kind of weirded me out.

Elissa and I would make out in one of our beds a lot, but that was just about all I could get out of her. Every time we would start making out, I would almost immediately get a boner. I'd be rubbing her tits, and it would just pop right up. I would grab her hand while we were making out and try to put it on my cock, but she would normally pull it away.

Finally, one day, she started rubbing my hard cock, but she would only do it over my shorts. I would pull my shorts and boxers down, but she would pull my boxers back up and keep rubbing it without actually touching it. She'd rub up and down my shaft until I would shoot my load in my boxers. I always hated this because then I would have cum all over my skin and in my pubes, and it was a bitch to clean up. I finally got her to actually jerk me off one day, but she didn't want to get cum all over her hand, so she put my dick back in my boxers when she knew I was about to cum.

The 4th of July was the first holiday we spent together as a couple. Now that I think about it, there must be something about that holiday that always gets me lucky. We spent the evening with my family watching the fireworks, and then Elissa asked me to come spend the night at her house because her parents were out of town.

While we were driving to her house, she told me that she wanted tonight to be the night. I was so excited when she said this because it had been a couple of years since the last time

I had sex. She told me she was nervous about getting pregnant, and I insisted that we would be fine with using condoms.

We got back to her house and went straight to her bedroom. I noticed that her brother's bedroom door was shut, which confused me because I thought everyone was gone. Elissa insisted that it would be fine and that he was probably in there banging his girlfriend. We walked into her bedroom, and I shut and locked the door behind me.

I wanted to slowly take her clothes off, but she beat me to it. She got into bed and kind of hid under the covers. It was cute, but I was already getting a boner and ready to go. I took my clothes off, jumped under the covers, and started making out with her.

We made out for a few minutes, and I started putting my finger in her pussy. She was so wet and started squirming as soon as I touched it. I started with one finger for a few minutes, and then slowly got a second one in there.

We kept making out, and then she went down to start sucking my dick. I have to admit, she was pretty terrible at it. I'm still not really sure what she was doing down there, but after two minutes I pulled her head back up towards mine to keep kissing her. I rolled over and grabbed a condom off the floor and started to put it on when she stopped me.

"Wait," she said. "I'm really scared I'm going to get pregnant." I assured her that the condom would be fine, but she was still nervous about it.

"What do you want me to do then?" I asked her.

"I don't know," she replied. I sat there for a minute, not really sure what to do, and then I had a genius idea. I threw on my boxers and ran out of the room.

I ran to the kitchen and started rummaging through the drawers. I was getting frustrated because I couldn't find what I was looking for. I went through every drawer and had to have been making a ton of noise. Thankfully, her brother never came out of his room.

Imagine me in the kitchen in my boxers with a rock-hard cock poking out–not really sure how I would have explained myself.

Finally, in the very last drawer, I found what I was looking for–saran wrap. I grabbed it and went running back into the bedroom. Elissa gave me a crazy look and asked what I was going to do with saran wrap. "I'm double wrapping my dick. There's no way you're getting pregnant tonight."

I'm not sure how, but I was still rock hard at this point. I was determined to get my nut. I tore off a piece of saran wrap and wrapped it around my hard dick. I then opened up a new condom and put it over the saran wrap. It felt a little weird, but I really didn't care.

I got on top of her and she helped me slowly guide my throbbing cock into her tight pussy. I barely even got the head inside of her, and she started moaning. I pushed it in, slowly, until the entire thing was in. It felt a lot different than the first time with Jane, probably because I didn't use a condom with her. Elissa was making some pretty weird faces, and I knew she was in a bit of pain. I was determined to get this over with as quickly as I could.

I pushed my cock in and out of her tight pussy pretty slowly, trying not to hurt her. She was grabbing onto my back pretty hard, and I felt her nails go into my skin a few times. Her pussy was so wet, and it felt so good, I could feel her pussy juices starting to get everywhere. I knew I wasn't going to last very long, and after about four minutes, I came in my saran condom. Elissa asked why I stopped, and I kind of laughed and told her I had finished. She pushed me off of her and got up and ran out of the bedroom, naked. I assumed she went running to the bathroom to wash up or something. As I laid there, I went to pull the condom off my still-hard dick, and it was super wet. I pulled the condom off and threw it on the floor, and when I looked at my hand, it was red. Blood.

Did I really fuck her that hard? Or is that what happens when a girl loses her virginity? Obviously, Jane wasn't a virgin when I fucked her in the shack.

Elissa came back into the room, and I asked her if she was okay. She must have gone into the bathroom to wipe the blood off her pussy. She looked at me and nodded her head "yes" and grabbed her cell phone. I asked if she was ordering pizza because I was hungry, and she said she was calling her mom.

She dialed her mom's number, and when her mom answered, Elissa said, "Mom, where's the tampons?"

Chapter 6

SEAN

Elissa and I were together for a few good years, but she really could be quite the bitch. During my second year of college, I became really good friends with a guy named Oliver, and he was in a similar situation with a super bitchy girlfriend. We kind of talked each other down off a ledge and made a decision that we both wanted to be single for a while. One night, I called Elissa and told her it just wasn't working out, and we broke up.

Breaking up was the best decision of my life. I was in my third year of college, going out every night and partying. The lease on Oliver's apartment was ending, and I was still living at home with my parents, so we decided to get an apartment together. At the same time, we both decided to take a semester off from school and just party and travel. We would literally find any reason we could to have friends over and throw a party. The Grammy's are on tonight? We had to have a party. The news was on at 6pm? We had to have a party. This whole thing turned out to be one of the best decisions I had made.

About this same time, I really started to question my own sexuality. Did Elissa and I break up because she was a bitch? Or did we break up because I just wasn't really that into her? I found myself starting to be super attracted to the male body, but thought maybe that was just because I wanted ripped muscles and a six-pack. I had been having thoughts since I was in my teens that I might be gay, but always just brushed it off as a phase because in the end I loved all the sexual experiences I'd had with two women.

Oliver was a very attractive man. He was about six feet tall, skinny and muscular. He's what the gay world would call a twink, but with muscles. His arms had these veins that would pop out like no other, and he had a smile that would make you melt. Even though Oliver had a girlfriend when we met, I still had my suspicions.

Oliver and I decided to take a trip to Florida to visit my sister, and then from there we went to the Bahamas for a few days. We went shopping before we left, and he bought a little empty bottle that could be used to put a liquid or a gel in. I wasn't really sure what he was getting it for, but I thought maybe he wanted to hide lube in it. We went on the trip, and I secretly was waiting, and wishing, for something to happen, but nothing did.

A few months later, we went on another trip to Phoenix, and again he bought the same bottle before we went. And again, nothing happened on the trip.

Looking back, I wish I just would have said something because I still think there was an attraction between us, and I think we were both scared to say something. We still keep in touch with each other, but he's married now, so there's that.

After coming back from that trip to Phoenix, I decided it was time to see what these feelings were that I had been having. It wasn't as easy back then to find a random hook-up as it is now, and I certainly wasn't going to go to the gay bar to find one. I didn't even know if I was gay, and I sure didn't want to run into anyone at the bar. So I started looking at the best place there was to find a hook-up: Craigslist.

I created a new email account just to use on Craigslist. I was so scared of someone finding out about what I was doing, or even worse, talking to someone on Craigslist who knew me. I must have spent over a month emailing guys. Most of the people I would talk to were old, horny men who weren't attractive at all. I wouldn't have minded an older guy showing me the ropes, but I needed him to at least be somewhat attractive.

I started emailing back and forth with this guy named Sean. He was a nurse and was only a few years older than I was. He was super cute, at least in the photos he had sent me, and had a pretty nice-sized cock. It wasn't as big as mine, but for what could potentially be my first one, I didn't mind.

We emailed back and forth for about a week, and I told him that I only wanted to make out and suck some dick. He kept saying he wanted to fuck me, but I wasn't ready for that. I told him that I would gladly fuck him, but he said he didn't bottom. I actually had to look that up because I wasn't sure what that meant. Little did I know, but there's guys who will only do one position and refuse to do the other.

Selfish.

Oliver was out of town visiting his family one weekend, and I decided to go out with some friends. I was pretty wasted, and when I got back home, I decided to message Sean and see if he wanted to come over. He quickly responded, and told me that he would have to bring his boyfriend with him.

What? Boyfriend? What the fuck.

Had I been sober I probably wouldn't have even responded because I surely didn't want my first time to be a threesome. But I said whatever, and twenty minutes later they were walking in my front door.

Sean walked in first. He was just as cute as he was in the pictures and was actually pretty muscular. His boyfriend, though, was another story. He was pretty overweight, and light blonde hair that was combed over to one side, and I didn't quite understand how the two of them were together. I offered them a drink and made myself a double because I was definitely going to need it. We made small talk in the kitchen for a little bit, and Sean's boyfriend told me that he was just there to watch. Not sure why, but I insisted that he join in.

After a few minutes of talking, we made our way to my bedroom. Sean sat down on the bed, and I walked right over to him and started making out with him. I'm not even sure what his boyfriend was doing, and quite frankly, I really didn't care.

As we were making out, Sean took his shirt off and then pulled mine off, and he pulled me closer so he could start kissing my neck.

Holy shit.

Kissing a guy was so much better than kissing a girl. I noticed out of the corner of my eye that his boyfriend had sat on the top part of the bed near the pillows and was rubbing his dick through his pants. I was still standing in front of Sean, and he quickly took my belt off and pulled my pants down. Naturally, my cock was already pretty hard, and he started sucking on it through my underwear. That really wasn't doing much for me, so I pulled my briefs down and grabbed the back of Sean's head, so I could force my cock in his mouth.

Fuck if he wasn't the best cocksucker I had ever had, not that I had many to compare to. He put my cock all the way in his mouth, and I could feel it squeeze down his throat. He started stroking my cock while he was sucking it, and every once in a while, would go down and suck on my balls while he continued to stroke my cock. That was a new feeling I hadn't felt before, and I loved every second of it. After a few minutes, I wanted to take a turn and see what he was working with.

Sean was still sitting on the bed, and I got down on my knees and pulled his pants down. I wasn't about to mess with the whole "suck it through the underwear." I just wanted it in my mouth. His cock was a lot bigger than it was in the photos, and it was pretty thick. I licked the tip of his head for a few seconds just to get a taste, shut my eyes, and started to go to town on his cock. He already had a ton of pre-cum dripping out, and it tasted so good.

After about thirty seconds of sucking his cock, I all of a sudden felt something on mine. I was a little surprised when I opened my eyes and looked down to see his boyfriend sucking on my dick. It was a way more intense feeling to be getting your dick sucked while sucking another one.

We kept going for a few minutes and I heard Sean say, "Please let me fuck you."

"Not happening," I responded. He begged for a few more minutes and I just kept saying no in between taking giant licks at his dick.

A few more minutes passed, and Sean told me he was getting close. I wasn't ready to take a cum shot to the face or the mouth yet, so I said, "Let's make out and jerk off."

We laid down on the bed next to each other and continued making out while stroking our cocks. His boyfriend went down and would take turns sucking on our balls while we were jerking off. Sean was stroking with his right hand and had his left hand squeezing one of my nipples, which felt really good.

About ten seconds later, I yelled out, "I'm gonna cum!" and for some reason got the idea to get up on my knees and shoot my load all over Sean's chest. I figured he would like this. I must have shot the biggest load I had ever shot in my life, and the minute my cum splashed on his chest, he started shooting his load. He had a pretty good cum shot, and his first shot even went up and hit his chin.

We sat there for a minute, not really saying anything, and I went and grabbed a towel. I wiped off my dick, and then handed him the towel to clean himself up.

We did that whole awkward "Goodbye— see you soon" thing, and they left. I went back into my bedroom and laid down in bed, wondering what I had just done. Even though it felt really good, I didn't feel good about it, and I don't think I enjoyed it.

Damn, maybe I wasn't gay.

A few days later, I woke up one morning with a giant sore on my lip. My first though was, "That mother fucker gave me herpes!"

I was livid.

I immediately called him and absolutely flipped the fuck out because we had talked about STD's, and he assured me he was completely clean.

"If you're clean, then why do I have a giant herpe on my lip?" I screamed at him.

He insisted he was clean, and a week later, the sore was gone and never came back. I guess it was just a cold sore, which I was prone to getting.

Still, it scared the fuck out of me.

Chapter 7

MY BOSS

A few months after my man-on-man blowjob, Elissa and I got back together. I felt pretty confident being with her and was certain that I wasn't gay. I ended up proposing to her, and she said yes. I told her about a girl that I hooked up with a few times while we were broken up, and she absolutely flipped out. So, for obvious reasons, I never told her about my incident with Sean because she would have been absolutely disgusted and definitely would not have gotten back together with me.

A couple years passed, and things were pretty normal, but our sex life really wasn't the greatest. For some reason, I was starting to have "those" feelings again and wasn't really sure what to do about them. I loved Elissa and didn't want to hurt her again. I wasn't about to go experiment again with another guy to figure things out, so I thought I could just bury it deep down inside, and eventually it would all go away.

That was, until, I met Thomas.

Thomas was my boss in the store that I worked at. He was a year older than I was, and just your typical charismatic cute guy. I had heard a few rumors that he had been with men, but then also heard rumors of other female managers in the store that he had hooked up with, so it was pretty confusing. He was always really nice to me, and of course, I always confused niceness with flirting, as I was never really good at telling the difference.

I really wanted to get to know Thomas better but wasn't really sure how to ask him to hang out. One day he was in the front of the store talking to me, and he randomly mentioned that he was going to be moving in a few weeks. I immediately knew this was my way in and wrote my phone number on a piece of paper with the offer to help him pack or move. He took the number and put it in his pocket, and I figured I was never going to get a call of text from him, so I kind of just let it be.

A few weeks later, I was going out of town with my dad. My parents had bought a car for Harry, and my dad needed me to drive it back for him. While we were on the way I got a text message from a number I didn't recognize.

To my surprise, the text message read, "Hey, it's Thomas. What's up?"

Was this real? Was he really texting me?

He sure was. We made a lot of small talk, talking about work, his move, and one of the girls he had hooked up with. We started talking about a party from a few months back, which is where I had heard that he had been with some guys. I was trying to get it out of him, when one of his texts read, "Well, I made out with two people, one of which may have been a guy, so…" That was exactly what I was looking for. I finally got him to say it. This was my chance.

We kept texting for the rest of the day. I told him that I was curious myself. He asked about my girlfriend, and I told him that things weren't going very well. I told him that I wanted to experiment, and that I felt like I'd be comfortable experimenting with him. He just said, "I'd be cool with that," and we kind of just left it there.

Over the next few months, we never really said anything more. Then, I decided to break up with Elissa.

Major things always seem to happen to me on holidays. It was New Year's Eve, and I was at Elissa's house with Oliver and a few other friends. Elissa was being a complete bitch, so my friends and I left and went to a bar. When we got back, she was in her bedroom, and I walked in and looked at her and she said, "I think we're done."

I responded with, "I think you're right." I leaned in to give her a kiss on the cheek, but she turned away from me. I left her house, and we never spoke again. It was the fastest, cleanest break-up in the history of break-ups. But this way made it so much easier to move on.

A few weeks later, I was texting Thomas and told him what had happened, and he asked me to come over to his apartment. I was kind of surprised but secretly very excited.

I went over, and he gave me a little tour. It was a pretty tiny second floor apartment, but I guess it was okay for him and his roommate. We walked back into the living room and Thomas looked at me in a very sexual way. He slowly made his way over to me, kind of like in the movies, and ever so slowly pressed his lips against mine. It was actually really romantic.

We stood there in his living room for a good five minutes making out in the same place, rubbing our hands all over each other's bodies. He pulled me close and pressed his hard cock against mine and started rubbing them together through our pants. He then turned and threw me down on the couch.

He pulled his pants down to unveil a cock that was almost identical to mine. He got down on his knees in front of me and pulled my pants down, grabbed my cock and put the entire thing in his mouth.

Wow, he was so much better than Sean was at it. He slobbered up and down on my cock for quite a while, and then stopped sucking it for a while to lick on of his fingers. He started sucking on my cock again, and I felt him pressing his finger against my hole. I wasn't sure

I was ready for it, but his wet finger slowly going deeper and deeper into my ass felt really good.

By the time he got his finger all the way in, he left it there for a few seconds and then started thrusting it in and out while he continued to suck on my dick.

This was a completely new feeling, and it hurt and felt amazing at the same time. I knew I wasn't going to last long, and about twenty seconds into it, I started shooting my load down his throat. I didn't even get a chance to give him a warning because it happened so quickly, and he gagged a little bit. I imagine it was a pretty big cum load. Aside from having a finger up my ass, I hadn't jerked off in about five days.

Thomas swallowed every last drop and stood up in front of me with his hard cock in my face. He pulled my head towards his dick and shoved it in my mouth. He started thrusting his hips and pumping his cock in and out of my mouth, and after about thirty seconds, he said that he was going to cum. I wasn't sure what to do, but since he took my load, I figured I should take his load. He pulled his cock out of my mouth to jerk it off, but I grabbed it and put it back in my mouth. I kept sucking on it like a champion when I felt that warm liquid shoot straight down my throat. I immediately started gagging, but I kept going until I got every left drop. It actually tasted pretty good, and I kind of made a vacuum with my mouth as I let his dick fall out, so I ensured I got every last drop. I stood up in front of him, and we made out for a few more minutes, and then he asked me to come back over the next day.

Naturally, I said yes.

Chapter 8

THOMAS & THE MOVE

I went back over to Thomas's place the next day, expecting that we would just be making out and sucking each other off again. At this point, I wanted to suck dick every day. I walked into his apartment, and he immediately started kissing me. I didn't even have time to take off my jacket. He grabbed my hand and led me to his bedroom.

He pushed me down on the bed and continued making out with me. We were rolling around, grabbing each other's dicks and kissing pretty passionately. To date, this was the most passionate experience I'd had.

We took each other's shirts and pants off and rolled around naked, sucking on each other's cocks and licking each other's balls. Thomas laid down with his head on the pillow and told me, "Come here." I was on my knees, and he motioned for me to come up toward his face. I straddled his face, facing the wall, and started to put my cock into his mouth. To my surprise, he kind of lifted me so that my ass was on top of his mouth, and then I felt it–his tongue was inside my hole.

Now this was a new amazing feeling I hadn't imagined before. Thomas was licking my hole, and I grabbed onto my cock and started stroking it. I felt his tongue go in and out of my hole, and then he would lick all around it. After about three or four minutes, I got off his face, and I'm not sure what came over me, but I told him I wanted him to fuck me.

I rolled over and laid down on the bed, and Thomas got on top of me. He spit in his hand and rubbed it all over his cock, and then spit again and rubbed it on my hole. I assumed we'd use lube, but really didn't care at this point. I also noticed that he didn't grab a condom, which I also didn't even care. I just wanted his cock inside of me.

He lifted my legs over his forearms and slowly rubbed the head of his cock on my hole, which felt really good. The minute his head entered, I immediately felt an extreme amount of pain. But it wasn't necessarily a bad pain. It hurt, but it didn't, if that makes sense. Thomas was very gentle, and it took a good minute before his cock was all the way inside of me. I still remember what my facial expressions must have looked like to him because I know my eyes and mouth were wide open. Luckily, the room was fairly dark.

He left his cock inside of me for a minute to let me get used to it. He then started moving it in and out very slowly, and fuck if it wasn't the most amazing feeling I had ever felt. As time went on, he went faster and faster, and it felt amazing. I started stroking my cock, which only added to the pleasure. He would lean down and kiss me while he was fucking me, and then go back up and say things like, "You like my cock, huh?"

No, I didn't *like* his cock–I *loved* his cock.

This went on for about ten minutes when I could tell I was about to cum. I wasn't even really stroking my cock anymore, but I could feel it happening. He grabbed my dick and started stroking it while he was still fucking me. The minute I started shooting my load on my chest Thomas let out a loud moan, and he made a few hard thrusts with his cock in my ass. I knew he had just cum inside of me, and I was actually pretty excited about it. We had cum at the same time, which was super hot.

We jumped in the shower together, made out a little more, and then I left.

A couple week later, Thomas called me and admitted that his roommate was actually his boyfriend. I was a little pissed at first, but honestly didn't care because the sex with Thomas was so good. Thomas told me he wanted to be with me, broke up with his boyfriend, and a month later, I moved in with him.

Thomas and I were together for three years. During those three years, we had a lot of threesomes and foursomes, which were always exciting until they were over; that's when I felt like shit. Come to find out, Thomas would then go and fuck some of these people without me, and without me knowing, as I never would have been okay with that. Thomas was addicted to sex, and even though I knew he was cheating on my while we were together, I would turn a blind eye and deny that it was happening.

Enough was enough. After three years of being together, we split up. Shortly after we split up, I was out with my friends at a gay bar watching a drag show. After the show, one of the drag queens who I had never even seen before walked up to me and randomly said, "I'm sorry."

"What are you sorry for?" I asked.

He responded, "Sorry I slept with your boyfriend while you were together."

At this point, I shouldn't have cared, but I was so fucking pissed. I wasn't really pissed that he had slept with Thomas. I was pissed that he had the audacity to walk up to me and say this, like it was really going to resolve anything or cleanse him of his wrongdoing.

Now this drag queen was nothing to special to look at and was an even uglier man out of makeup. I had never felt the urge to punch someone, but when he said this to me, I could feel my fist clench up, and I pulled my arm back, almost to get some momentum to really knock this bitch out. Just as I swung my arm back, I felt my friend grab it, and I immediately dropped it. Being a pretty witty person, I just replied by saying, "Wow, I see he's downgraded," and I walked away.

I knew it was time to leave Intercourse and move onto something bigger and better. I quit my job at the practice I was working at, packed my car with whatever I could fit into it, said goodbye to my family, and headed west for California. I didn't really know where I was going or what I was going to do when I got there.

What I did know, though, was this was about to be an epic adventure that I probably wouldn't be able to write home about.

Author Bio

Grayson Ace has had his fair share of sexcapades, and figured why not write about them?   Recently divorced, he is re-discovering himself (and plenty of hot men) and creating many new sexy adventures along the way. If you like what you see, please leave a review, and you never know....you may end up in one of the stories!

GraysonAce.com
Facebook: Grayson Ace
Instagram: graysonaceofficial
Twitter: @GraysonAce1

MORE BOOKS FROM GRAYSON ACE

First Year Out of the Closet
You're Only a Top?

9 781644 500675